A Note from Michelle about
HOW TO MEET A SUPERSTAR

Hi! I'm Michelle Tanner. I'm nine years old, and I just got elected class president. Now it's time to start working on my promises. But I made one promise that's going to be tough to keep.

I told the whole fourth grade that the Ginger Girls would sing at our school. But I was wrong. Now everybody says that if the Ginger Girls *don't* come to our school I can't be president.

My family can't even help me with this problem. I wish they could because I have a *very* big family.

There's my dad and my two older sisters, D.J. and Stephanie. But that's not all.

My mom died when I was little. So my uncle Jesse moved in to help Dad take care of us. So did Joey Gladstone. He's my dad's friend from college. It's almost like having three dads. But that's still not all!

First Uncle Jesse got married to Becky Donaldson. Then they had twin boys, Nicky and Alex. The twins are four years old now. And they're so cute.

That's nine people. And our dog, Comet, makes ten. Sure, it gets kind of crazy sometimes. But I wouldn't change it for anything. It's so much fun living in a full house!

My Class
by Michelle Tanner

Jewel

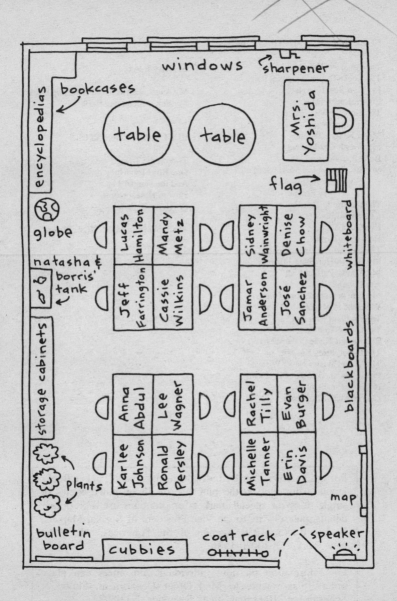

FULL HOUSE™ MICHELLE novels

The Great Pet Project
The Super-Duper Sleepover Party
My Two Best Friends
Lucky, Lucky Day
The Ghost in My Closet
Ballet Surprise
Major League Trouble
My Fourth-Grade Mess
Bunk 3, Teddy and Me
My Best Friend Is a Movie Star!
    (Super Special)
The Big Turkey Escape
The Substitute Teacher
Calling All Planets
I've Got a Secret
How to Be Cool
The Not-So-Great Outdoors
My Ho-Ho-Horrible Christmas
My Almost Perfect Plan
April Fools!
My Life Is a Three-Ring Circus
Welcome to My Zoo
The Problem with Pen Pals
Tap Dance Trouble
The Fastest Turtle in the West
The Baby-sitting Boss
The Wish I Wish I Never Wished
Pigs, Pies, and Plenty of Problems
If I Were President
How to Meet a Superstar

Activity Books

My Awesome Holiday Friendship Book
My Super Sleepover Book

FULL HOUSE™ SISTERS

Two on the Town
One Boss Too Many
And the Winner Is . . .
How to Hide a Horse
Problems in Paradise

Available from MINSTREL Books

FULL HOUSE™

Michelle

and Friends

HOW TO MEET A SUPERSTAR

Jacqueline Carrol

A Parachute Press Book

A MINSTREL® BOOK

Published by POCKET BOOKS
New York   London   Toronto   Sydney   Singapore

A MINSTREL PAPERBACK *Original*

A Minstrel Book published by
POCKET BOOKS, a division of Simon & Schuster Inc.
1230 Avenue of the Americas, New York, NY 10020

A PARACHUTE PRESS BOOK

Copyright © and ™ 2000 by Warner Bros.

FULL HOUSE, characters, names and all related indicia are trademarks of Warner Bros. © 2000.

ISBN: 0–671–04195–9

First Minstrel Books printing January 2000

10 9 8 7 6 5 4 3 2 1

A MINSTREL BOOK and colophon are registered trademarks of Simon & Schuster Inc.

Cover photo by Schultz Photography
Clothing on cover courtesy of Space Kiddets

Printed in the U.S.A.

PHX/

HOW TO MEET A SUPERSTAR

Chapter

1

♥ "Being class president is so cool!" Michelle Tanner declared. She smiled excitedly and crossed the school yard with her two best friends—Mandy Metz and Cassie Wilkins.

It was Wednesday. One week after Michelle was elected president of the fourth grade. She had some really great ideas. And she couldn't wait to start working on them.

"Uh-oh. Look." Cassie pointed across the school yard. Rachel Tilly stood on the steps

1

with her best friend, Sidney Wainwright. Both of them frowned at Michelle.

Michelle sighed. "Rachel is still angry because I won and she didn't."

"She's just a sore loser," Mandy said. "Everybody knows you'll be the best president. That's why they voted for you."

Erin Davis and Jeff Farrington ran up to them. "Hey, Michelle, did you talk to the Ginger Girls?" Jeff asked.

"We can't wait for them to get here!" Erin cried.

The Ginger Girls were a totally awesome singing group. They were giving three concerts in San Francisco. After Michelle was elected president she promised to get them to sing at Fraser Street Elementary.

Michelle had promised a lot of things during her campaign. Getting the Ginger Girls was definitely the most popular promise, though.

"They get into town tomorrow," Erin said. "What day are they coming to our school?"

Before Michelle could answer, three more kids gathered around her. All of them wanted to know about the Ginger Girls.

"I hope they'll sign autographs," Denise Chow said.

"I want to get my picture taken with them!" Lee Wagner added.

"This is so great, Michelle," Anna Abdul told her. "I couldn't get tickets to any of their concerts, but now it doesn't matter."

The bell rang. Michelle, Cassie, and Mandy hurried toward the school doors.

"Hey, wait up!" Victor Velez cried. He caught up to Michelle and her friends.

Victor had run for president, too. Michelle was impressed with a lot of his ideas, so she asked him to be her vice president.

"Hi, Victor." Michelle pulled a sheet of paper out of her pink and blue backpack. "I

3

made a list of some of the things for us to work on." She handed him the paper.

"More school trips," Victor read. "More books and videos in the library. Wrap-a-Lunch Day." He paused. "What's that?"

"You know those sandwiches called wrappers?" Michelle said. "It would be great if one day a week, the cafeteria people put out the wrapping bread and all kinds of fillings. Then everybody could make one."

"Cool idea!" Victor agreed. He glanced at the list again. "What about the Ginger Girls? They're not on here."

"Don't worry," Michelle told him. "I didn't forget about them. My uncle Jesse is a musician. His friend Tom plays guitar for the Ginger Girls. Tom said he'd get them to come to our school."

"Awesome!" Victor cried.

Michelle and her friends hurried inside. School hadn't even started, but Michelle couldn't wait for it to be over. Today was the day Tom would call Uncle Jesse—to say when the Ginger Girls would sing at Fraser.

After school Michelle ran all the way home from the bus stop. Her strawberry-blond hair bounced up and down as she rushed into her house. Comet, the Tanner family's golden retriever, trotted over to Michelle.

"Hi there, Comet." Michelle scratched the dog behind the ears. "Have you seen Uncle Jesse?"

Comet licked her hand and wagged his tail.

Footsteps pounded on the stairs. Michelle's sister, Stephanie, hurried into the living room.

Michelle had two sisters—Stephanie and D.J. Stephanie was in eighth grade. D.J. was in her first year at college. D.J. had her own bedroom, but Michelle and Stephanie shared one.

That was because the Tanner house was very full. Besides Michelle and her sisters, there was their father, Danny. Uncle Jesse and his wife, Becky, lived on the third floor. They had four-year-old twins named Nicky and Alex.

That wasn't everyone, though. Joey Gladstone was Danny's best friend, and he lived in an apartment in the basement. He moved in to help out after Michelle's mom had died.

Last but not least, Michelle had a new guinea pig named Sunny. He lived in a cage in Michelle's room.

Michelle liked living in a house with eight other people, a golden retriever, and a guinea pig. There was always somebody to talk to. Right now, though, the only person she wanted to talk to was her uncle.

"Have you seen Uncle Jesse?" she asked Stephanie.

"He's in the kitchen with the twins," Stephanie answered. "They spilled some juice. They're trying to clean it up before Dad gets home."

Michelle smiled. She knew her dad would not be angry about the spilled juice, but he did like to keep the house super clean. He would probably mop and wax the whole kitchen floor if he saw the mess.

Stephanie pulled on a green sweatshirt and yanked open the front door. "I'm going over to Allie's to study. Don't forget, it's your turn to set the table for dinner tonight!"

Michelle plopped her backpack on the couch. Then the twins ran out of the kitchen.

"Hi, Michelle," Alex said. "We helped clean up the floor."

"Now we can play!" Nicky shouted. The boys dashed up the stairs.

Michelle hurried into the kitchen. "Uncle Jesse, did you find out about the Ginger Girls?" she asked excitedly.

"I sure did." Jesse threw a wad of paper towels into the garbage can. "And I have good news."

7

"Yes!" Michelle pumped her fist in the air.

"But . . ." Jesse held up his hand. "I also have some bad news."

Bad news? Uh-oh. Michelle didn't like the sound of that!

Chapter

2

♥ "What do you want to hear first?" Jesse asked. "The good news or the bad news?"

"Um . . . the good," Michelle decided.

Jesse grinned. "You're looking at a guy who can get four tickets to the Ginger Girls concert on Sunday afternoon," he said. "And you and your two best friends can be my dates."

"Uncle Jesse, that's awesome!" Michelle cried. "Wait until I tell Cassie and Mandy. They're going to flip! Thank you, thank you, thank you!"

"Well, it's the least I can do," Jesse said.

"What do you mean?" Michelle asked.

"Remember, I have some bad news, too." Jesse took a deep breath. "My friend Tom couldn't get a meeting with the Ginger Girls. So he couldn't ask them to sing at your school. He tried, but it's just impossible. He's really sorry, and so am I."

Michelle felt her heart sink. She didn't blame Uncle Jesse. If his friend couldn't ask the Ginger Girls to sing at Fraser Elementary, then Michelle would have to break her most popular promise to the fourth grade.

This isn't bad news, she thought. This is a disaster!

The next morning at the bus stop, Michelle told Cassie and Mandy the good news—that Uncle Jesse got them tickets to the concert.

"All right!" Cassie shrieked. "Did you hear

that, Mandy? We're actually going to see the Ginger Girls live!"

"It's so cool!" Mandy cried. "Super, super cool!"

Cassie and Mandy were so excited, they hopped up and down. Then Michelle told them the bad news—that Uncle Jesse's friend didn't ask the Ginger Girls to sing at their school.

"Oh, no!" Cassie groaned.

"I wish I never made that promise," Michelle said. "How am I going to tell the other kids that I can't keep it?"

"But it isn't your fault," Mandy told her.

The bus arrived, and Michelle and her friends climbed on. Almost everyone started shouting questions at Michelle. Questions about the Ginger Girls.

"What day are they coming to the school?"

"How many songs will they sing?"

"Will we get to meet them?"

Michelle sighed. She wanted to tell everybody the bad news, but she didn't know how. Everyone will be so disappointed, she thought.

Rachel got on at the next stop. She took the seat across from Michelle.

Michelle groaned to herself. When Rachel hears that the Ginger Girls aren't coming, she'll blame me!

Finally things got quieter. Everyone waited for Michelle to say something. But she just couldn't tell them the bad news. It was too hard!

Michelle took a deep breath. "Listen, everybody," she called out. "I know you're all excited about the Ginger Girls. But there are lots of other things to get excited about, too. I have a really cool idea for a Wrap-a-Lunch Day. And I'm going to write a letter that says the fourth grade should be able to use the new fifth-grade playground. If everybody signs it, I'll bet—"

"Come on, Michelle, we don't want to hear about that stuff!" Evan Burger said loudly.

"Yeah. We want to know about the Ginger Girls," Lee agreed.

"Gin-ger Girls! Gin-ger Girls!" Jeff shouted.

Everyone took up the chant. Everyone except Rachel.

Rachel waited for the noise to stop. Then she flipped her long brown hair over her shoulder. "Michelle hasn't answered a single question about the Ginger Girls," she said. "You know what? I bet they're not coming. I bet they never *were* coming."

"What are you talking about?" Erin asked.

"Michelle was just showing off," Rachel declared. "She promised us the Ginger Girls so we'd all think she's a great president. "But she's not *really* going to keep that promise."

Everyone looked at Michelle.

"Is that true, Michelle?" Jeff asked.

"No!" Michelle shook her head. "When I made that promise, I meant it. Honest!"

"I don't believe you." Rachel sneered. "I think you're totally lying."

"Well, you are totally *wrong!*" Michelle insisted. Now she knew she couldn't tell the bad news. If she did, everyone would think she *was* a liar.

Besides, she was president. She didn't want to let the other kids down. She had to keep her promise. If Uncle Jesse's friend couldn't get the Ginger Girls, then Michelle would have to do it herself.

Michelle sat up straight. She looked Rachel right in the eye. "I promised to get the Ginger Girls, and I will," she said. "Just wait and see!"

Chapter 3

♥ "I have to keep my promise," Michelle told Mandy and Cassie. The three friends were hurrying to Michelle's house after school. "But I need your help. We have to figure out a way for me to talk to the Ginger Girls."

"You could write and ask to meet them," Mandy suggested. Then she frowned. "No. That's no good. They must get thousands of fan letters every day."

"Besides, the mail will take too long,"

Michelle agreed. "They'll be in town only a few days."

"What about a fax or an e-mail?" Cassie asked. "Those would be super fast, right?"

"Right," Michelle said. "Except the Ginger Girls probably get lots of faxes and e-mails, too. Mine would just get lost in a huge pile. But there has to be a way!"

"Don't worry," Cassie told her. "We'll think of *some*thing."

Michelle led the two girls into her house. Nicky and Alex were watching cartoons in the living room.

"Let's go into the kitchen," Michelle told her friends. "Dad made some of his special chocolate chip-oatmeal cookies. Maybe they will help us think."

"Look, Michelle," Nicky cried. He pointed to the television. "It's the Ginger Girls!"

Michelle stopped and stared. The cartoon was over. A news break was on. The picture showed the four Ginger Girls waving and smiling as they climbed into a long, white limousine. A large crowd of people stood behind a fence. They cheered and waved back at the singers.

"More than two hundred fans turned out to greet the Ginger Girls at the airport," a voice on the television announced. "This mega-hot singing group will give three concerts while they're here. And tickets are already sold out."

Now the picture showed the limousine slowly pulling away. "As the Ginger Girls headed toward the Fairmont Hotel, some of their fans had to be kept from jumping on the car," the announcer continued. "Ginger fever is climbing. We don't expect it to go down anytime soon."

That's it! Michelle thought. She knew just how she would talk to the Ginger Girls.

"Come into the kitchen," Michelle told

Mandy and Cassie. "I have to use the phone."

"What for?" Mandy asked as they walked into the kitchen.

"I'm going to call the Fairmont Hotel," Michelle explained. "The news said the Ginger Girls are staying there. I don't have to write or fax them. I can pick up the phone and *call* them!"

Keeping her promise wouldn't be impossible after all. Michelle was sure the Ginger Girls would sing at her school once she asked them. Uncle Jesse's friend said they were really nice.

Michelle flipped through the Yellow Pages and found the Fairmont Hotel. She picked up the phone and dialed the number. "It's ringing," she told Mandy and Cassie.

Cassie and Mandy crossed their fingers.

"Fairmont Hotel," a man's voice answered. "How can I help you?"

Michelle took a deep breath. "Hi. My name

is Michelle Tanner. I'd like to talk to the Ginger Girls, please."

"Oh?"

"Yes. I have a *very* important question to ask them," Michelle told him. "I really, really need to talk to them."

"Sure, kid," the man chuckled. "You and about a zillion other fans. Sorry. I can't put your call through."

"But—" Michelle started to say.

Click! Then a dial tone buzzed in Michelle's ear.

"I can't believe it!" she cried. "He hung up on me!"

Chapter

4

♥ "What a creep!" Cassie said. "I can't believe he hung up."

Michelle sighed. "I guess hundreds of fans have been calling the hotel." She put her head in her hands and groaned. "What are we going to do now?"

"Don't give up yet," Mandy told her. "We'll figure something out. Let's eat some cookies and think about it."

"Good idea." Michelle grabbed the cookie jar from the counter. She pulled out a cookie for each of them. Then they sat at the kitchen table, eating and thinking.

When the first cookie was gone, they had two more. And they kept thinking.

Soon it was time for Mandy and Cassie to go home. They still didn't have a single new idea.

"You can still send an e-mail," Cassie said as she and Mandy stepped out onto the front porch. "Who knows? Maybe the Ginger Girls will actually read it."

Michelle nodded. "I guess that's what I'll do. Thanks for trying to help, guys. See you tomorrow."

Michelle went into the living room. Her stomach hurt from eating too many cookies. Her brain hurt from not having any good ideas. She plopped down on the couch with a big sigh.

If I can't get the Ginger Girls, I'll have to tell the whole fourth grade, she thought.

Rachel will say I lied about everything. And the other kids will be really disappointed.

I can't go back on my promise, she decided. I'm president. I have to get the Ginger Girls. I just have to!

Uncle Joey bounded into the room with a basketball tucked under his arm. "Hey, Michelle, what's with the serious face?"

"I'm thinking," she told him. "Very, very hard."

The front door opened. Danny walked in with a huge smile on his face. "Have I got news for you," he announced. "I'm going to interview the Ginger Girls on my talk show tomorrow!"

Danny hosted a TV show every morning. It was called *Wake Up, San Francisco.*

"Way to go!" Joey told him.

Michelle couldn't believe it. This was the perfect chance for her. She jumped up from the couch. "Dad, please take me with you," she cried. "It would be so cool if I could meet them!"

Michelle didn't want to tell her father about the mess she was in. She wanted to fix things herself. After all, that's what a president was supposed to do, right?

"I could get their autographs and everything," Michelle told Danny. "I could actually talk to them!"

Danny frowned. "I don't know, tomorrow's a school day."

"I know, but this is important," Michelle argued. "I don't have a test or anything. And I could go back to school after lunch."

"I don't think cutting school is a good idea," Danny said. "Even if it is only a half-day."

"That's not what you thought in college," Joey told Danny with a laugh.

"Dad cut school?" Michelle asked.

Joey's eyes sparkled. "Your dad and I were major fans of Bruce Springsteen," he

23

explained. "And when we heard he was giving a concert a hundred and fifty miles away, we hopped in my old clunker and drove there as fast as we could."

Danny chuckled. "What a ride! The car shook like crazy every time Joey took it over forty miles an hour."

"But we made it," Joey reminded him. "We saw Springsteen live. *And* we cut a whole day of classes to do it."

Michelle looked at her father with hopeful eyes. "Please, Dad . . ."

"Come on, Danny, lighten up," Joey urged. "It won't hurt if Michelle misses one day of school."

"Well . . ." Danny hesitated.

Michelle crossed her fingers.

"Okay," her father said. "But just this once."

"Thanks a lot, Dad! Thanks, Uncle Joey!" Michelle gave them both a big hug. Then she raced toward the kitchen. "I'm going to call

Cassie and Mandy and tell them the good news!"

"Tell them to write down your morning assignments, too," her father reminded her.

"I will," Michelle promised. "Thanks again, Dad. This is so great!"

I'm going to talk to the Ginger Girls, she thought. I won't have to break my promise, after all!

Chapter
5

♥ Michelle and her father walked into the TV station at six o'clock the next morning. *Wake Up, San Francisco* started at seven.

"The Ginger Girls aren't here yet," Danny told Michelle. "I have to talk to the director for a minute, okay?"

"Okay, Dad." Michelle sat in a chair and waited.

She had been to the station before, but she had never seen everyone so excited. Everyone was talking about the Ginger Girls. They couldn't believe such a famous group was going to be on their show.

Michelle was excited, too. She was also a little nervous. This was her big chance to ask the Ginger Girls to sing at her school. Probably her only chance.

"Okay, Michelle." Danny walked up to her. "I just got word that the Ginger Girls are here," he said. "Let's go say hello."

Thank goodness, Michelle thought. It was twenty minutes to seven. There wasn't a lot of time left before the show started. She would have to talk fast.

"Where are they?" she asked as they headed down a hallway.

"In the greenroom," Danny answered. "That's what we call the room where the guests wait to go onstage. There's a telephone if they need to make calls. And they can have coffee, tea, and doughnuts."

Danny stopped in front of a door. He gave it a quick tap, then pushed it open.

Michelle took a deep breath and followed him inside.

The four Ginger Girls looked up and smiled.

Lulu's purple hair stood up in spikes. May and Gigi were twins, with curly red hair. Tawny wore her long black hair in a loose top-knot. It spilled down her head like a water fountain.

Michelle's heart began to pound. She suddenly felt very nervous. It's really them, she realized. It's really the Ginger Girls. I'm actually here with the most famous singing group in the whole wide world!

"Good morning," Michelle's father said. He crossed the room and shook hands with the Ginger Girls. "I'm Danny Tanner, the host of *Wake Up, San Francisco*. It's great to have you on our show."

"Thanks, we're glad to be here," Lulu told him. "This is our first time in your beautiful city. We love it."

"Love the doughnuts, too," Tawny said with a grin. "We were starving!"

Everyone laughed. Then Gigi peered over Danny's shoulder at Michelle. "Who's this?" she asked with a friendly smile.

"This is my daughter, Michelle," Danny explained. He waved his arm. "Michelle, meet the Ginger Girls."

"Hi, Michelle," the four singers said.

Michelle felt her mouth curve into a big grin. She tried to speak. But nothing came out! She swallowed hard. "It's so . . . you're so . . . this is so . . . cool!" she blurted out in a squeaky voice.

Danny put his arm around Michelle's shoulders. "Michelle's a big, big fan of yours," he told the group.

Michelle nodded her head up and down.

The Ginger Girls smiled.

Don't just stand here, Michelle told herself. Ask them to sing at the school! She swallowed again. "Uh . . . see . . . I wondered . . ."

The Ginger Girls kept smiling. They seemed really nice.

Michelle could tell they wouldn't mind if she asked them to sing at her school. She was so excited about being in the same room with them, she could hardly speak, though.

Danny put a hand on Michelle's shoulder. "I think someone's a little star struck."

Everyone laughed again.

Michelle blushed. She was so embarrassed. Try again, she told herself. She cleared her throat. "I . . . uh . . . I have a . . ." she started to say.

Someone rapped on the door. "Five minutes, everybody!" a voice called out.

"Well, we'd better get onstage," Danny said. He went to the door and held it open.

The Ginger Girls rose from their chairs and

hurried across the room. "Bye, Michelle!" they called out. Then they were gone.

Michelle squeezed her eyes shut and blew out a big puff of air. Then she flopped down on to a couch.

How could I *do* that? she wondered. My one big chance to talk to the Ginger Girls. And I totally blew it!

Chapter
6

♥ "I still can't believe I froze up," Michelle moaned. "What a total disaster."

It was Friday afternoon. The class was just getting back from lunch. Michelle, Cassie, and Mandy were gathered around Michelle's desk. They were talking about the Ginger Girls.

Mandy shook her head. "I probably wouldn't be able to talk to them, either. They're so famous and everything."

"It's too bad you couldn't find them after the TV show," Cassie said.

"I know." Michelle nodded. "But they left the second it was over."

Mandy sighed. "Are you going to tell the class about it?"

"Not yet," Michelle told her. "There has to be something else we can do."

"Yeah!" Cassie agreed. Then she frowned. "Like what?"

"I don't know," Michelle admitted. "But I'm not ready to give up. As long as the Ginger Girls are in town, I'm going to try to see them again."

Victor came over to Michelle's desk. He looked excited. "Guess what?" he asked. "I talked to the head cafeteria lady about Wrap-a-Lunch Day. She thought it was a good idea."

"That's great!" Michelle said.

"She wants us to write the idea down and give it to her," Victor explained. "Then she'll talk it over with the cooks."

"All right!" Michelle cried. "One of my ideas is really going to happen. Thanks, Victor."

Victor smiled. "Hey, what about your biggest idea?" he asked. "Did you find out when the Ginger Girls are coming?"

"Yeah!" Rachel plopped her books on her desk. Her seat was next to Michelle's. "What *about* the Ginger Girls, Michelle?"

Michelle looked around. More kids had filed into the classroom. All of them were gathering around her.

The Ginger Girls will probably be in town until Sunday, Michelle reminded herself. It's not too late to get them.

"What's the matter, Michelle?" Rachel asked in a snippy voice. "Don't you have an answer?"

"As a matter of fact, I don't," Michelle admitted.

Everyone gasped.

"Not *yet,*" Michelle added quickly. "The Ginger Girls are very busy right now."

"Well, when will they tell you?" Rachel demanded.

"As soon as they can," Michelle answered. As soon as I ask them, she thought. I *hope*.

Most of the kids looked satisfied. Rachel crossed her arms and frowned. "I don't believe you," she said.

"Me, either," Sidney agreed. "I don't think the Ginger Girls will *ever* come to Fraser."

"Yes, they will!" Cassie insisted.

"Yeah," Lee said. "I believe Michelle."

"Me, too," Anna declared.

"So do I," Erin agreed. "Michelle wouldn't make a promise she couldn't keep."

Michelle felt great that so many kids were sticking up for her. She couldn't let them down. She *would* get the Ginger Girls!

"I don't care what Michelle says," Rachel said. "The Ginger Girls are *not* coming to Fraser."

"You want to bet?" Cassie asked.

"Sure," Rachel said. "What about you, Michelle?"

"Yes!" Michelle cried. "I'll bet anything!"

"Good. Then if the Ginger Girls come to Fraser, I'll take back everything I said about you," Rachel told her. "But if they *don't* . . . you have to quit being president of the fourth grade!"

Chapter 7

♥ "Why did I ever make that stupid bet?" Michelle groaned after school that day. "If I can't get the Ginger Girls now, I'll be going back on a promise—*and* I won't get to be president anymore."

"Don't give up yet," Cassie said as the three friends walked into the Tanner house. "We'll think of a way for you to see the Ginger Girls again."

"I'm not giving up," Michelle told her. "But

we have only two days. We better think fast."

The three friends climbed the stairs to Michelle's room. Mandy and Cassie sat on the floor. Mandy propped her chin in her hands, frowning hard. Cassie leaned against a wall and wrapped her arms around her knees.

Michelle curled up on her bed and pulled Mr. Teddy onto her lap. The teddy bear was her favorite stuffed animal. Holding him made her feel better.

It didn't give her any ideas, though.

Fifteen minutes passed. Cassie sighed. "I can't think of anything."

"Me, either," Michelle admitted. "But we have to keep trying. It's not like the Ginger Girls are a thousand miles away. They're right here in town."

"That's it!" Mandy cried. She jumped to her feet. "The Ginger Girls are in town. They're staying at the Fairmont Hotel!"

Cassie nodded. "Sure, but Michelle already tried to call them, remember?"

"I know, but why should she call them, when they're right here in San Francisco?" Mandy asked.

"You're right." Michelle hopped off the bed. "We should go to their hotel!"

Mandy nodded. "They've already met you. I bet they'll see you if you go there in person."

"It's a great idea!" Cassie cried.

"It's perfect," Michelle agreed. "Come on. I think D.J. was downstairs when we came in. Let's see if she'll take us."

The three girls raced downstairs. But D.J. wasn't around. She must have gone out, Michelle thought.

Stephanie was in the backyard playing with Comet, but she couldn't drive. Nobody else was home.

"Now how are we going to get there?"

Michelle asked. "I'm not allowed to take a bus or taxi by myself."

"Look!" Cassie pointed out the front window. "Your aunt Becky just pulled into the driveway."

"Great!" Michelle said. "Maybe she'll take us. Let's go ask."

They ran outside. Aunt Becky was just climbing out of the car.

"Aunt Becky, I need your help," Michelle told her.

"It's important," Cassie said.

"Super important," Mandy added.

"Whoa!" Aunt Becky held up her hands, laughing. "I get the picture. What do you want me to do?"

Michelle quickly explained about going to see the Ginger Girls at the Fairmont Hotel.

Aunt Becky thought a few seconds. "Well, I just dropped the twins off at a birthday party. I'm free. So . . . why not?"

"Do you mean it?" Michelle asked. "You'll really take us?"

"Sure." Aunt Becky laughed again. "When I was seventeen, a bunch of friends and I practically camped out in the parking lot of the Fairmont one night. We were dying to get Jimmy Prince's autograph."

"Who?" Cassie asked.

"He was a famous rock star," Becky explained. "Way back in the Dark Ages, when I was a teenager."

"Did you get his autograph?" Michelle asked.

Becky shook her head. "We didn't even catch a glimpse of him. All we got was cold and sleepy. But I never regretted it. And I know how much you want to see the Ginger Girls. So let's go!"

Michelle gave her a hug. "Thanks, Aunt Becky."

Cassie and Mandy quickly called home and

got permission to go. Then everyone piled into Becky's car.

This *has* to work, Michelle thought as they drove away. Mandy was right. The Ginger Girls will remember me from yesterday. I'm sure they'll see me.

Of course, she wasn't sure they would sing at her school. But Michelle couldn't worry about that yet. First things first, she thought.

The car suddenly slowed down.

"Uh-oh," Becky said. "I should have thought of this." She pointed out the window.

Michelle looked. Her heart sank.

A huge crowd of people was gathered in front of the Fairmont Hotel. Some of them wore Ginger Girls T-shirts. Others held posters with the singers' pictures on them. A few even carried radios that blared out the group's songs.

"I guess you're not the only fans who

decided to come to the hotel," Becky said.

Michelle's heart sank even lower. "Look at them all. We'll never even get inside."

"Never say never." Aunt Becky grinned. "Stick with me. I have an idea!"

Chapter 8

♥ Becky gripped the steering wheel. She changed lanes and turned on to a side street.

"What's your idea, Aunt Becky?" Michelle asked. "Do you know a secret way into the hotel or something?"

Becky shook her head. "It's not a secret. But maybe nobody else thought of it. Keep your fingers crossed."

Michelle crossed her fingers as Becky turned around another corner.

Now they were driving down a bumpy

alley. A big delivery truck was parked on one side. Garbage cans and Dumpsters lined the other side. There wasn't a person in sight.

"Great!" Becky said. "I think this just might work."

"Where *are* we?" Cassie asked.

"At the back of the Fairmont," Becky told her. She stopped the car behind a big blue Dumpster. "All right, everybody out and follow me."

The three girls climbed out and walked behind Becky. They headed down the alley.

"Your aunt is so cool," Mandy whispered to Michelle.

Michelle smiled. She knew that was true.

Becky stopped in front of a door. It was held open with a heavy brick. Delicious cooking smells floated into the alley.

"Oh, I get it," Michelle said. "We're going through the kitchen, right?"

"Right," Becky replied.

"Wow—you really know your way around this place," Cassie said.

Becky laughed. "I should. I spent almost a whole night here once, remember? Okay, now, listen. Walk fast, but don't run. Don't act like you're sneaking around. And don't talk to anybody. Ready?"

"Ready!" the girls said.

"Then, let's go!"

Becky stepped through the doorway. Michelle, Cassie, and Mandy followed close behind her.

The kitchen was big, noisy, and busy. Three cooks in white jackets and tall white hats stood at a long metal counter. They were chopping vegetables. Three more stood in front of huge stoves. They were stirring and frying things and shoving pans into the ovens.

Waiters rushed in and out. They carried silver trays high above their heads.

Michelle thought for sure somebody would yell *stop!* Hardly anyone even glanced at them. They were all much too busy.

It took only a minute for Becky and the girls to make their way to the far side of the kitchen. They hurried through a set of double doors and into a hallway.

Becky glanced around. Then she tilted her head to the right. "This way," she whispered.

They set off down the hall. A couple of minutes later, Becky pulled open a door that led to the lobby. "Mission accomplished," she declared.

The four of them stepped into the big lobby. It was decorated with gold-framed mirrors and red velvet chairs.

It also had *a lot* of people in it.

Becky shook her head. "This place is like a zoo. Sorry, guys."

"It's not your fault, Aunt Becky," Michelle told her. "Anyway, I'm still going to try to see

47

the Ginger Girls." She spotted the check-in desk. That's where she wanted to go.

Cassie leaned close to Michelle. "What do we do now?"

Michelle grabbed Cassie's hand. "Come on."

"Excuse me . . . excuse me!" Michelle and Cassie repeated over and over. They had to move around so many people. Bellboys in short red jackets. Men and women with brief-cases.

And fans. Lots and lots of Ginger Girls fans.

Finally they reached the other side of the lobby. Michelle smoothed back her hair and straightened her clothes. She stood on tiptoe to see over the top of the desk.

"Excuse me," she called out.

The man behind the desk turned around and smiled politely. "Yes? May I help you?"

"You sure can." Michelle smiled back. "Could you please ring the Ginger Girls' room and let them know Michelle Tanner is here?" she asked.

The man raised an eyebrow. "What was the name again?"

"Michelle Tanner. T-a-n-n-e-r," she told him.

He pulled a sheet of paper from behind the desk. He glanced at it and frowned. "You're not on the list," he said.

"What list?" Cassie asked.

"The list of visitors," he answered.

"Well, that's because they didn't know I was coming," Michelle explained. "But I'm sure they'll see me. All you have to do is tell them I'm here."

The man shook his head. "Miss, do you have any idea how many Ginger Girls fans have tried to trick me into calling their room or giving out their room number?"

"We're not trying to trick you," Cassie argued. "See, we're not fans. Well, we are, but . . ."

"I'm sorry, girls," he told them. "I can't help you."

"Please . . ." Michelle started to say.

Just then a group of fans rushed up to the desk.

"Yikes!" Michelle and Cassie jumped out of the way.

Then another group of people crowded around them.

Cassie gasped as a man's briefcase thumped her in the arm. "Ouch!"

"I'm sorry," the man said. "Are you all right?"

Cassie rubbed her arm. "Sure."

"Whoa!" Michelle cried as someone else bumped into her. "Let's get out of here, Cassie. This place could be dangerous to our health." She stumbled sideways and swung her arm out. It banged against something and glass rattled loudly.

"Careful," a voice warned.

Michelle caught her balance and looked around. She and Cassie were in front of the elevators. Michelle had bumped into a big room-service cart covered with a long white cloth. The cart had a silver pot, a plate of cookies, and four china cups on it.

"Sorry," Michelle told the bellboy standing next to the cart.

"It's okay. Nothing got broken or spilled, thank goodness." The bellboy pushed an elevator button. "The last thing I want is to mess up the Ginger Girls' tea!"

The Ginger Girls' tea?

Michelle wished she could take the cart up to them.

Cassie nudged Michelle in the arm. "Remember that movie we saw on TV last Saturday?" she whispered. "You know, the one where the man needed to get out of his hotel room. But the bad guys were waiting outside for him."

"He hid in the serving cart," Michelle whispered back. "The bad guys never had a clue." Then she smiled. "I could do the same thing!" But how can I get under the cart without the bellboy seeing me? she wondered.

Michelle glanced at the bellboy. He was staring at the numbers above the elevator door.

"Excuse me, young man." A woman tapped the bellboy on the shoulder. She was holding a tiny white poodle with a pink bow in its curly fur. "Where can I find some dog biscuits for my Misty? She's hungry."

"Yap, yap, yap!" the dog barked. Then it leaped from the woman's arms.

"Misty!" the woman cried.

"I'll get her." The bellboy chased the poodle down the hallway. The woman followed close behind.

"Now's your chance," Cassie told Michelle. "I'll go find Mandy and your aunt Becky."

She glanced down the hallway. "Hurry, Michelle!"

Michelle lifted the white cloth on the cart. Then she quickly crawled on to the shelf at the bottom. The long cloth hung down, hiding her from sight.

"Yap, yap, yap!" Michelle heard the poodle's bark coming close again.

"Stop, pooch!" the bellboy shouted.

"Misty, sweetie," the woman called. "Come back here."

Then suddenly a wet black nose poked through a gap in the cloth. Misty stuck her head under the room-service cart. Her brown eyes zeroed in on Michelle.

"Yap!" the poodle barked. "Yap, yap!"

Michelle gasped. What was she going to do?

Stop barking, Misty! she thought at the dog. Be quiet! You're going to give me away!

Misty barked again.

53

"Misty, you silly doggie!" the woman cried.

"Hey, pooch, what did you find under there?" the bellboy asked.

Michelle held her breath. If he looked under the cart, it was all over!

Chapter

9

♥ Michelle squeezed her eyes shut. Please don't find me, she wished with all her might. She opened her eyes—and saw a pair of hands pull Misty away.

"Don't pay any attention to her, young man," the woman said. "She just smells the cookies. Misty is always looking for food, aren't you, sweetums?"

Misty whined.

"No, I'm not going to put you down," the woman said to her dog. "We're going to get you some real oatmeal cookies. Forget the dog biscuits."

Misty's whines grew softer as the woman walked away.

Michelle silently let her breath out. That was close!

Ping! Michelle heard the elevator doors whoosh open. She clung to the shelf as the cart began to roll. The doors closed. The elevator began to rise.

Michelle's heart pounded. She tried not to breathe or make a sound. The elevator rose higher and higher.

Ping! The doors opened. The bellboy shoved the cart out. He rolled it down a hall. Then the cart jerked to a stop.

We must be at the Ginger Girls' room, Michelle thought excitedly.

The bellboy rapped on a door. "Room service!" he announced.

The door opened.

Wham! Someone bumped into the serving cart.

"Hey!" The bellboy gasped. He yanked the cart aside so hard that Michelle almost fell off the shelf.

"I'm so sorry!" someone said. Michelle recognized Lulu's voice. "We tried to call, but we missed you. We won't have time for tea, after all."

"Yes, we have another interview," Tawny said. "I'm afraid we have to leave this very second."

"Busy, busy, busy!" Lulu laughed.

What? The Ginger Girls were leaving? Michelle peeked through the gap in the cloth.

Sure enough, she saw four pairs of legs rushing down the hall. They turned a corner and vanished from sight.

The bellboy slowly rolled the cart back to the elevator.

I was so close to talking to them! Michelle

57

thought as they rode down. Now what am I supposed to do?

The elevator stopped and the doors opened. The bellboy rolled the cart out.

"Young man!" a woman called out breathlessly. It was Misty's owner. "Misty got away from me again. She's heading for the main door. Please, stop her!"

"Yes, ma'am!" the bellboy cried. He shoved the cart against a wall. Michelle saw his legs running through the crowd.

She quickly climbed out from under the cart and stood up.

"Michelle!" Cassie shouted. "Over here!"

Michelle slowly made her way across the crowded lobby, where Aunt Becky and her friends were waiting.

"Guess what?" Cassie exclaimed. "The Ginger Girls just went through here a minute ago, and we saw them!"

"Lulu was so close, I could have touched

her," Mandy said. "I said her name and she smiled at me!"

"Really? Did you ask her about singing at the school?" Michelle asked.

Mandy shook her head. "I couldn't. They were in a hurry."

"Where did you go, Michelle?" Becky asked. "I was getting worried."

"I'm sorry," Michelle told her. "I was trying to see the Ginger Girls. But I missed them. I didn't even see them go through the lobby."

"I know you're disappointed." Becky put her arm around Michelle's shoulders. "Maybe they'll come to town again sometime."

Maybe, Michelle thought. But it will be too late then.

As they left the lobby, Michelle saw the bellboy again. He carried Misty in his arms. Misty was still yapping.

Becky dropped off the three girls at

Michelle's house. Then she drove away. She had to pick up the twins.

Michelle, Mandy, and Cassie went inside and plopped down on the couch. "I have only two days left!" Michelle said desperately. "Time's running out. Does anybody have any ideas? Because *I* don't!"

"I don't, either," Mandy admitted.

"Me, either," Cassie said. "At least, not yet."

Jesse burst in from the kitchen. "I thought I heard your voices," he said. "And you're just the people I want to see."

"What's going on?" Michelle asked him.

"Ta-da!" Jesse pulled four small pieces of paper from his shirt pocket. He waved his hand and bowed from the waist. "Allow me to present you with . . . tickets to the Ginger Girls concert. This Sunday afternoon!"

"Wow!" Mandy cried. She jumped up from the couch. "Thanks, Mr. Katsopolis. This is awesome!"

"We're really going to the concert!" Cassie exclaimed. She bounced up and down on the couch. "I can't believe it!"

Michelle gave Jesse a big hug. "Thank you, Uncle Jesse. You're the coolest uncle I know."

Michelle could hardly wait for Sunday. She really wanted to hear the Ginger Girls sing, and that wasn't all.

Going to the concert gave her one more chance to talk to the Ginger Girls—her *last* chance.

Chapter
10

♥   "One more song!" the crowd roared. "One more song!"

The four Ginger Girls stood on the stage. Their red dresses were covered with sequins that glittered in the spotlights. They smiled and waved to the thousands of screaming fans in the audience.

Michelle sat in an aisle seat four rows from the stage. Cassie sat next to her, then Mandy, then Jesse. The concert was so great that the audience didn't want the Ginger Girls to stop. Not even for intermission.

Michelle could hardly wait for them to take a break. As soon as they did, she could put her plan into action.

"One more song!" the fans chanted. "One more song!"

Lulu held up her hands. "All right!" she cried. "You've talked us into it!"

The crowd clapped and whistled. Some of them began shouting out the names of songs they wanted to hear.

Michelle leaned close to Cassie. "It's time!" she said into her friend's ear.

Cassie poked Mandy in the arm. "It's time," she told her.

Mandy glanced at Jesse. He was on his feet, clapping and shouting. Mandy gave Michelle a thumbs-up signal.

The Ginger Girls started singing again. Michelle took a last look at Uncle Jesse. Then

63

she slipped into the aisle and started walking toward the stage.

Michelle's plan was simple. She would sneak into the Ginger Girls' dressing room and pop the question as soon as they walked in the door.

Mandy and Cassie would make sure Uncle Jesse didn't notice she was gone. He would definitely not like her sneaking around.

Michelle was desperate. She had to try.

Nobody paid any attention as Michelle made her way down the aisle. When she reached the bottom, she turned left. She spotted a door. It must lead backstage, she thought.

Then she saw a big man standing next to the door. His arms were crossed. He was watching the crowd.

I should have known there would be a security guard here, Michelle said to herself. Her shoulders slumped in disappointment. She turned away.

"Hey!" a man shouted in a deep voice.

Michelle turned back. The security guard was running toward her. Michelle's knees started to shake. But the guard rushed right past her. A bunch of fans were trying to jump onto the stage.

What luck! Michelle thought. She spun around and raced to the door. She pushed through it into a hallway. It was filled with microphones and cables. To her left she could see the Ginger Girls singing on the stage.

A group of workers stood near the stage, watching the show.

Michelle let out a cheer. "I did it! I'm backstage!"

A man from the group turned around. "How did you get back here?" he asked Michelle.

Michelle froze. "I . . . uh . . ."

"Come on, Jake. She probably has a pass," a woman from the group said. "It's not like she could have just walked in from the crowd, right?"

Jake nodded, then turned back to watch the show.

Michelle ran around the corner as fast as she could. "That was close," she whispered.

It was easy to find the right dressing room. The door had a big pink star on it. GINGER GIRLS was printed above it.

Michelle looked over her shoulder. Don't chicken out now. She took a shaky breath. Then she turned the doorknob and went inside.

Michelle gulped when she saw the room. Dressing tables with brightly lighted mirrors lined a wall. The tables were covered with combs and brushes and makeup. Flowers and fan letters were all over the place.

Michelle ran a hand across glittering costumes that hung on a rack. "This is so cool!" She plopped onto a soft cushy couch against a wall.

Michelle started to feel a little guilty. She knew that she shouldn't be there. Even worse, what if she got caught? What if Jake found out she didn't have a backstage pass?

Don't think about that, Michelle told herself. If you get *too* nervous, you'll freeze up again.

I'd better practice what I'm going to say to the Ginger Girls, she thought.

Michelle jumped off the couch and stood in front of a mirror. "I'm Michelle Tanner, remember me?" She cleared her throat. "I met you with my father at the TV station. And I—"

Michelle stopped. Had she just heard footsteps? She listened.

Yes! They were definitely footsteps. They were getting louder, heading toward the dressing room.

The Ginger Girls are on their way, Michelle thought. Her heart pounded like crazy. I'm finally going to get my chance!

Chapter

11

♥ The footsteps came closer. Closer. Then they stopped.

The Ginger Girls will be here any second, Michelle thought excitedly. Michelle took a deep breath.

"What does she look like?" a man's voice said outside the door.

"I wrote it down. Just a minute," a second man answered.

Michelle let her breath out. It wasn't the Ginger Girls, after all. They must have decided to sing another song, she thought.

"Here it is," the second man said. "Nine-year-old girl. Strawberry blond hair. Pink pants with butterflies on them. Black T-shirt. And a pink leather jacket."

The footsteps continued down the hall.

Michelle slowly turned her head and stared into one of the mirrors. Strawberry blond hair. Pink pants with butterflies on them. Black T-shirt. A pink leather jacket.

It's me! she realized. They were talking about me!

Uncle Jesse must have noticed I was gone, Michelle thought. She felt guilty. He's probably freaking out. She couldn't stay there and let him be worried.

Michelle started for the door. Then she had an idea. There was one last thing she could try.

A pile of fan mail lay on the coffee table. Michelle shook one of the letters out of its envelope. She took the envelope to a dressing table.

She found a pencil, and quickly wrote a note:

Dear Ginger Girls,

I met you with my father, Danny Tanner, at the TV station a few days ago. You may remember me because I couldn't say a word. I really wanted to. You see, I'm president of the fourth grade at Fraser Street Elementary. And I promised that you would sing at our school. Some of the kids think I was lying. But that's not true. My uncle's friend said you would probably do it. But then he couldn't get to ask you. I really hate to break my promise. That's why I'm inviting you to sing at my school. I know you're really busy.

But it would be so cool if you could come.

Love,
Michelle Tanner

P.S. Your concert was great! No matter what happens, I will always be one of your biggest fans.

Michelle drew a big heart after her name. Then she stuffed the note into the frame of the mirror.

This is definitely my last chance, she thought. If this doesn't work, I can kiss being president good-bye!

Chapter

12

♥ "I am very disappointed," Michelle's father told her. "How could you sneak off like that? You could have gotten hurt or lost."

The concert was over. Cassie and Mandy had gone home. Michelle was in the kitchen with her dad.

Danny wiped the counter with a sponge. "Didn't you realize how worried Uncle Jesse would be?" he asked. "Besides, you didn't have any right to go into the Ginger Girls' dressing room."

"But I really, *really* needed to ask them to come to the school," Michelle told him. "I promised the whole fourth grade that they'd sing."

Danny stared at her. "Why on earth did you do that?" he asked.

"Uncle Jesse's friend said that the Ginger Girls were really nice," Michelle explained. "He said that they would do it. But then he couldn't ask them. I tried to ask them at the TV station. But I was too nervous."

Danny sat at the table. "Why didn't you tell me, Michelle? I could have asked them for you."

"I wanted to do it myself," Michelle answered. "I'm the president. It's my job."

Danny smiled. "That doesn't mean you can't ask for help. Presidents ask for help all the time."

"I wish I had," Michelle admitted. "I tried to call the Ginger Girls, too. Then I tried to see them at the hotel and the concert. Nothing worked. Now it's too late. The Ginger Girls are leaving tomorrow!"

Danny pulled out a chair and sat next to Michelle at the table. "It's too bad it didn't work out. But you still shouldn't have sneaked away."

"I'm sorry," Michelle told him. "I won't do anything likc that again. I didn't mcan to worry Uncle Jesse. I told him I was sorry, too."

Danny patted her on the shoulder. "That's good," he said. "But I'm still going to have to ground you next weekend. No phone. No TV. No going anywhere."

Michelle nodded. "I wish I didn't have to go to school tomorrow." She sighed. "I'm going to have to tell everybody that the Ginger Girls aren't coming. And I won't be president anymore."

"Sure you will," Danny said. "Just tell

everyone the truth. Tell them exactly what happened. They'll know you didn't break your promise on purpose."

Maybe I didn't mean to do it, Michelle thought. But I still broke my promise. And I lost the bet with Rachel.

By this time tomorrow, I won't be president anymore.

"I knew you were lying!" Rachel declared loudly.

It was Monday morning, two minutes before class started. Mrs. Yoshida was talking to another teacher out in the hall.

Michelle was standing at her desk. She had just told the rest of the class that the Ginger Girls would not be coming to the school. Some of the kids looked angry. The rest of them looked disappointed.

"I wasn't lying. I can explain . . ." Michelle started to say.

"Ha!" Rachel rolled her eyes. "Why should we believe what you say now?"

"Because it's the truth!" Michelle declared.

"Big deal," Rachel said. "Anyway, you lose the bet, Michelle."

Michelle groaned to herself. She knew this was her own fault!

Mrs. Yoshida came in. "Good morning, class. Today, we're . . ."

The loudspeaker crackled noisily. "Attention," the office secretary said. "Will Michelle Tanner please come to the principal's office? Michelle Tanner to the principal's office."

Everyone stared at Michelle. She felt her face turn red. Getting called to the principal's office was definitely not good. This was turning out to be a very bad day.

"Here you go, Michelle," Mrs. Yoshida said. She handed Michelle a hall pass.

"You are in big trouble now," Rachel whispered to Michelle. "Just wait—I bet you're going to get suspended."

Michelle slowly walked to the principal's office. She twisted the hall pass in her hands. Her stomach kept doing flip-flops.

Was Rachel right? Michelle wondered. Would she really be suspended?

Chapter 13

♥ The principal's door was closed. Michelle felt like running away. But she slowly raised her hand and knocked.

"Come in!" Mr. Posey called.

Michelle took a deep breath and pushed open the door.

She couldn't believe her eyes.

Gathered around Mr. Posey's desk were . . . the Ginger Girls!

"Michelle!" Lulu cried. "Thanks so much

for inviting us. Mr. Posey has been telling us all about your school."

"Yes, we can't wait to sing for you," Gigi agreed. "It's going to be so much fun!"

"Uh . . . uh . . ." Michelle stammered. She still could hardly believe it. She kept staring.

It was the Ginger Girls, all right, dressed in black silk jumpsuits with silver fringe.

Tawny laughed. "Now, don't tell us the cat's got your tongue again!"

"You . . . you . . ." Michelle swallowed. "You mean you're really going to sing for us?"

"That's why we're here," May said with a grin. "When we found your note, we remembered you and your father right away. And we knew exactly how you felt about not breaking promises."

"We decided to help you keep yours," Lulu said.

"This is so cool!" Michelle cried. "It's

totally awesome. I can't believe it. Thank you!"

"We're glad to do it," Tawny told her. "We have just enough time before our plane leaves. And we're lucky—Mr. Posey agreed to let us sing during your assembly today. Isn't that sweet of him?"

Michelle had never heard anyone call Mr. Posey *sweet* before. She grinned at him.

Mr. Posey blushed. "Yes, well, we did have a dentist coming in to speak. But we can call another assembly about tooth care later," he said. "I don't think anyone will complain if we hear the Ginger Girls sing instead. Do you, Michelle?"

"Are you kidding?" Michelle asked. "This is going to be the most popular assembly in the history of Fraser Elementary!"

The Ginger Girls stood on the stage and blew kisses to the packed auditorium. "We're so glad to be here!" Tawny called into the microphone. "I can tell you're going to be one of the best audiences we've ever had!"

The entire fourth grade whistled and clapped and stomped their feet.

"This is so great!" Mandy shouted to Michelle. "I can't believe they're actually here!"

"Me, either," Michelle admitted. "I'm really glad I could keep my promise."

"And you get to stay as president," Victor said.

"And Rachel has to take back all the stuff she said about you!" Cassie declared.

"That's right!" Lee agreed. "Hey, Rachel! You should tell Michelle you're sorry."

"I'm *not* sorry," Rachel declared. "When Michelle made that promise, she didn't know if the Ginger Girls would come or not. That was cheating."

"It was not!" Victor argued. "Besides, I

think Michelle's going to be a great president."

"Apologize to Michelle, Rachel!" Lee shouted. "You lost the bet."

"Yeah!" the rest of the class agreed loudly.

Rachel crossed her arms and sighed. "Okay, I'm sorry," she admitted. "Now, could everybody please be quiet so we can hear the concert?"

Lulu stepped up to the microphone. "We have time only for a few songs," she announced. "And we would like to dedicate the first one to the person who invited us to your wonderful school—Michelle Tanner!"

Everyone shouted and clapped again. Then the Ginger Girls launched into their biggest hit.

Michelle bounced in her seat to the beat of the music. She was so happy. The kids didn't think she was a liar. She didn't have to quit being president. Most of all, Michelle kept her promise.

She glanced around at her classmates and smiled. It was turning out to be a great day, after all.

Don't miss out on any of
Stephaine and Michelle's
exciting adventures!

FULL HOUSE™
SISTERS

When sisters get together...
expect the unexpected!

A MINSTREL® BOOK
Published by Pocket Books

2012-03

FULL HOUSE™
Michelle

#8: MY FOURTH-GRADE MESS 53576-5/$3.99
#9: BUNK 3, TEDDY, AND ME 56834-5/$3.99
√#10: MY BEST FRIEND IS A MOVIE STAR!
(Super Edition) 56835-3/$3.99
#11: THE BIG TURKEY ESCAPE 56836-1/$3.99
#12: THE SUBSTITUTE TEACHER 00364-X/$3.99
#13: CALLING ALL PLANETS 00365-8/$3.99
#14: I'VE GOT A SECRET 00366-6/$3.99
#15: HOW TO BE COOL 00833-1/$3.99
#16: THE NOT-SO-GREAT OUTDOORS 00835-8/$3.99
√#17: MY HO-HO-HORRIBLE CHRISTMAS 00836-6/$3.99
MY AWESOME HOLIDAY FRIENDSHIP BOOK
(An Activity Book) 00840-4/$3.99
FULL HOUSE MICHELLE OMNIBUS 02181-8/$6.99
√#18: MY ALMOST PERFECT PLAN 00837-4/$3.99
#19: APRIL FOOLS 01729-2/$3.99
#20: MY LIFE IS A THREE-RING CIRCUS 01730-6/$3.99
#21: WELCOME TO MY ZOO 01731-4/$3.99
#22: THE PROBLEM WITH PEN PALS 01732-2/$3.99
#23: MERRY CHRISTMAS, WORLD! 02090-6/$3.99
#24: TAP DANCE TROUBLE 02154-0/$3.99
MY SUPER SLEEPOVER BOOK 02701-8/$3.99
#25: THE FASTEST TURTLE IN THE WEST 02155-9/$3.99
#26: THE BABY-SITTING BOSS 02156-7/$3.99
#27: THE WISH I WISH I NEVER WISHED 02151-6/$3.99

A MINSTREL® BOOK
Published by Pocket Books

It doesn't matter if you live around the corner...
or around the world...
If you are a fan of Mary-Kate and Ashley Olsen,
you should be a member of

MARY-KATE + ASHLEY'S FUN CLUB™

Here's what you get:
Our Funzine™
An autographed color photo
Two black & white individual photos
A full size color poster
An official **Fun Club™** membership card
A **Fun Club™** school folder
Two special **Fun Club™** surprises
A holiday card
Fun Club™ collectibles catalog
Plus a **Fun Club™** box to keep everything in

To join Mary-Kate + Ashley's Fun Club™, fill out the form
below and send it along with

U.S. Residents – $17.00
Canadian Residents – $22 U.S. Funds
International Residents – $27 U.S. Funds

MARY-KATE + ASHLEY'S FUN CLUB™
859 HOLLYWOOD WAY, SUITE 275
BURBANK, CA 91505

NAME: _Daniella Kazotti_

ADDRESS: _70 Brodway Street_

_CITY: _Chicopee_ STATE: _MAS_ ZIP: _01820_

PHONE:(_413_) _241-4088_ BIRTHDATE: _12/26_

1242

Split-second suspense...
Brain-teasing puzzles...

No case is too tough for the
world's greatest teen detective!

NANCY DREW®
MYSTERY STORIES
By Carolyn Keene

Join Nancy and her friends in
thrilling stories of adventure and intrigue

Look for brand-new mysteries
wherever books are sold

Available from Minstrel® Books
Published by Pocket Books

2313